HONEY...HONEY...LION!

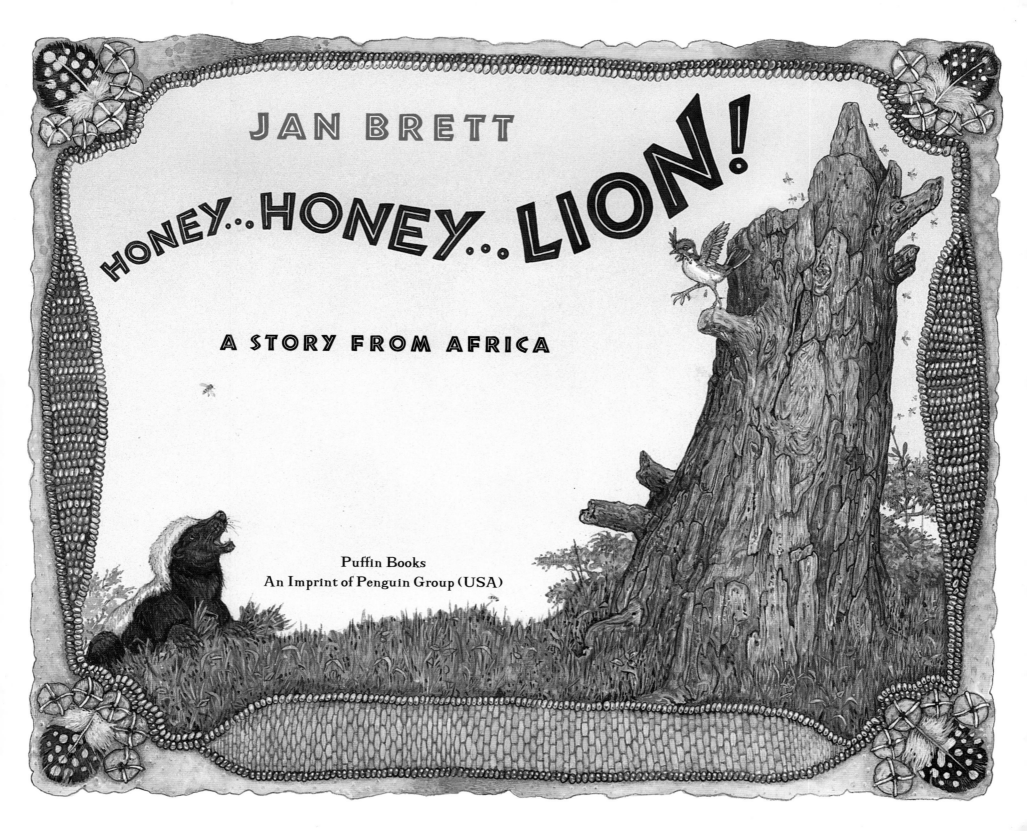

JAN BRETT

HONEY...HONEY...LION!

A STORY FROM AFRICA

Puffin Books
An Imprint of Penguin Group (USA)

To
Duduetsang Tiego

PUFFIN BOOKS
Published by the Penguin Group
Penguin Group (USA) LLC
375 Hudson Street
New York, New York 10014

USA * Canada * UK * Ireland * Australia
New Zealand * India * South Africa * China

penguin.com
A Penguin Random House Company

First published in the United States of America by G. P. Putnam's Sons,
a division of Penguin Young Readers Group, 2005
Published by Puffin Books,
an imprint of Penguin Young Readers Group, 2014

Copyright © 2005 by Jan Brett

THE LIBRARY OF CONGRESS HAS CATALOGED THE
G. P. PUTNAM'S SONS EDITION AS FOLLOWS:
Brett, Jan. 1949—Honey . . . honey . . . lion!: a story from Africa /
Jan Brett.
p. cm.
Summary: After working together to obtain honey, the African
honey badger always shares it with his partner, the honeyguide
bird, until one day when the honey badger becomes greedy and
his feathered friend decides to teach him a lesson.
ISBN 978-0-399-24463-6 (hardcover)
[1. Honey badger—Fiction. 2. Honeyguides—Fiction.
3. Symbiosis—Fiction. 4. Africa—Fiction.]
I. Title. PZ7.B75225Hon 2005 [E]—dc22
2005000449

Puffin Books ISBN 978-0-14-751352-6

Manufactured in China

7 9 10 8 6

IN AFRICA the honeyguide and the honey badger are partners when it comes to honey. The little bird follows a bee to its hive, and then she leads the honey badger there to break it open with its big strong claws. Together they share the sweetness. And that is the way it has always been.

Maybe this day Badger was hungrier than usual. Maybe he forgot about Honeyguide, who showed him the way.

Or could he have been thinking: My strong claws do all the hard work. Whatever the reason, that day Badger would not share.

Honeyguide scolded Badger as he waddled back to the Jackalberry tree, his tummy almost touching the ground. She fussed and fumed as he tried to fit into his burrow.

Finally she cried out for all the animals
to hear, "No fair, no fair!"
Soon all the guinea hens were broadcasting
the news, "Honeyguide is in a major rage!"

But Badger didn't hear. He was sound asleep, smiling, snoring and hiccuping from his big meal.

"Grrrrrr-umph!" Badger roared out the loudest hiccup of all, and its deep, low rumble gave Honeyguide an idea.

The next morning Badger woke up hungry, his tummy flat as a pancake. That's when Honeyguide flew by, heading for the great gray baobab.

"Honey, honey, honey!" she cried, grinning.

The little bird zigzagged over its large roots.

PITTER, PATTER!

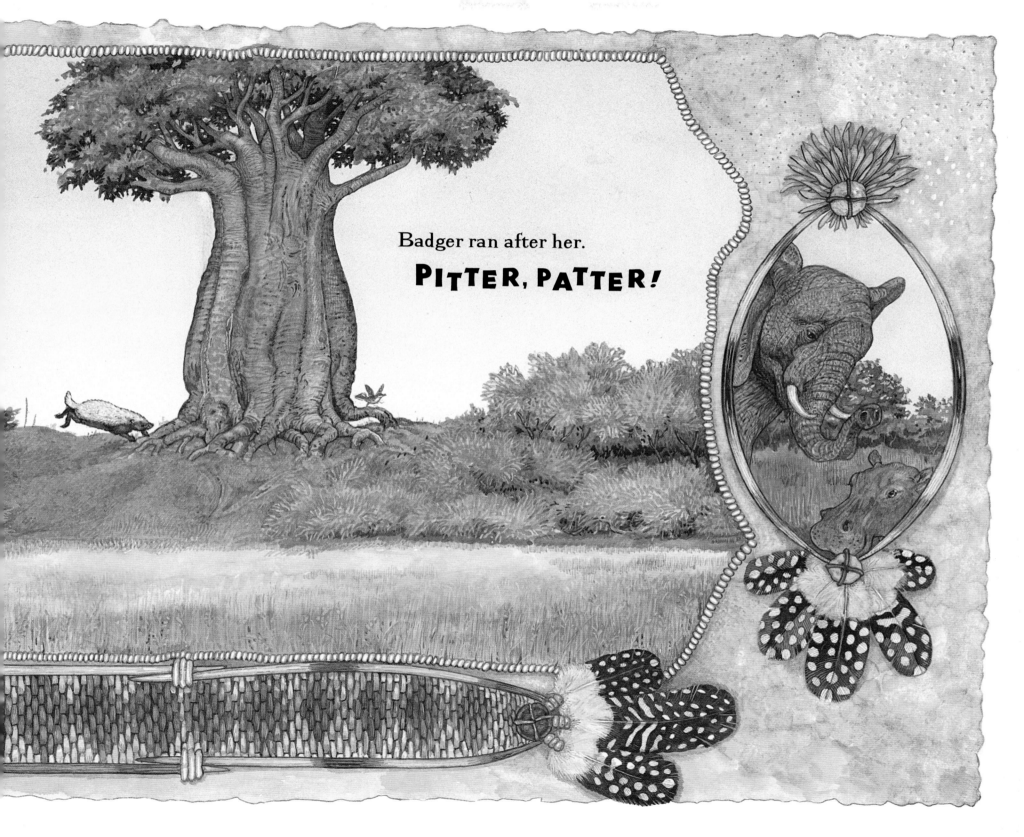

Badger ran after her.

PITTER, PATTER!

Honeyguide flew low across the water hole.

SPLISH, SPLASH!

Badger paddled after her.

SPLISH, SPLASH!

Honeyguide glided to the top of a termite mound and bounced on one foot. **SPRONG!**

Badger scrambled to the top
and bounced off.

SPRONG!

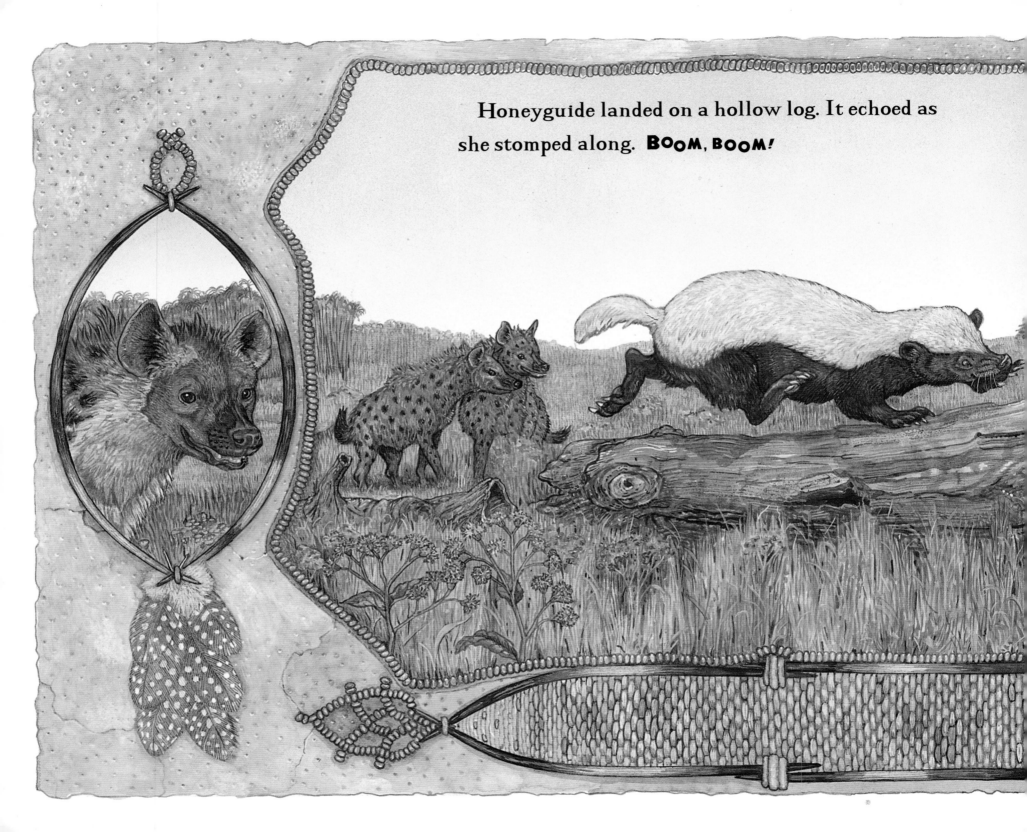

Honeyguide landed on a hollow log. It echoed as she stomped along. **BOOM, BOOM!**

Badger hurried to catch up. **BOOM, BOOM!**

Next Honeyguide flitted through a stand of papyrus. Tall, dry reeds waved back and forth. **CLICKETY-CLICK!** Badger traipsed along, muttering, "Where is that honey?" The papyrus rattled as he went by.

CLICKETY-CLICK!

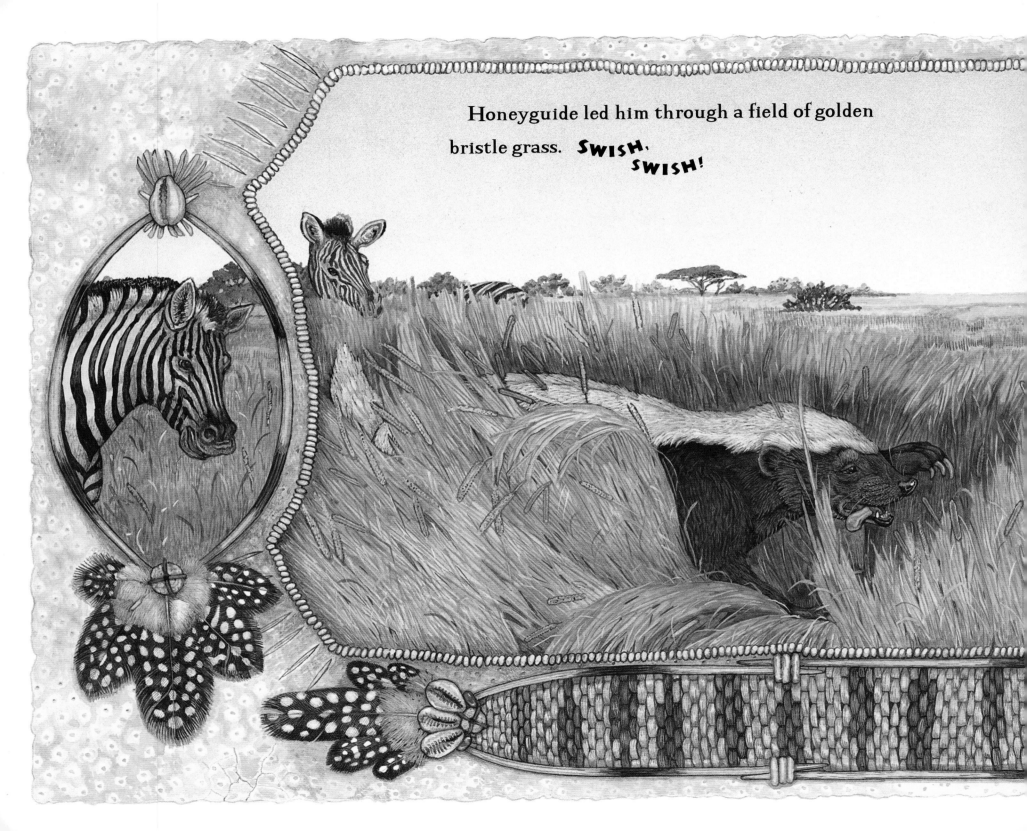

Honeyguide led him through a field of golden bristle grass. **SWISH, SWISH!**

Badger huffed and puffed, but the thought of
the delicious meal waiting for him kept him going.

SWISH,
SWISH!

By now Badger was tired and wet, itchy and sore. But he didn't slow down, because Honeyguide was just ahead of him. She flashed her wings, fanned her tail and dove under an acacia tree.

Badger charged in after her, singing triumphantly,

HONEY...HONEY...

LION, **LION, LION!**

Badger turned on his tail and ran.

SWISH, SWISH through the grass . . .

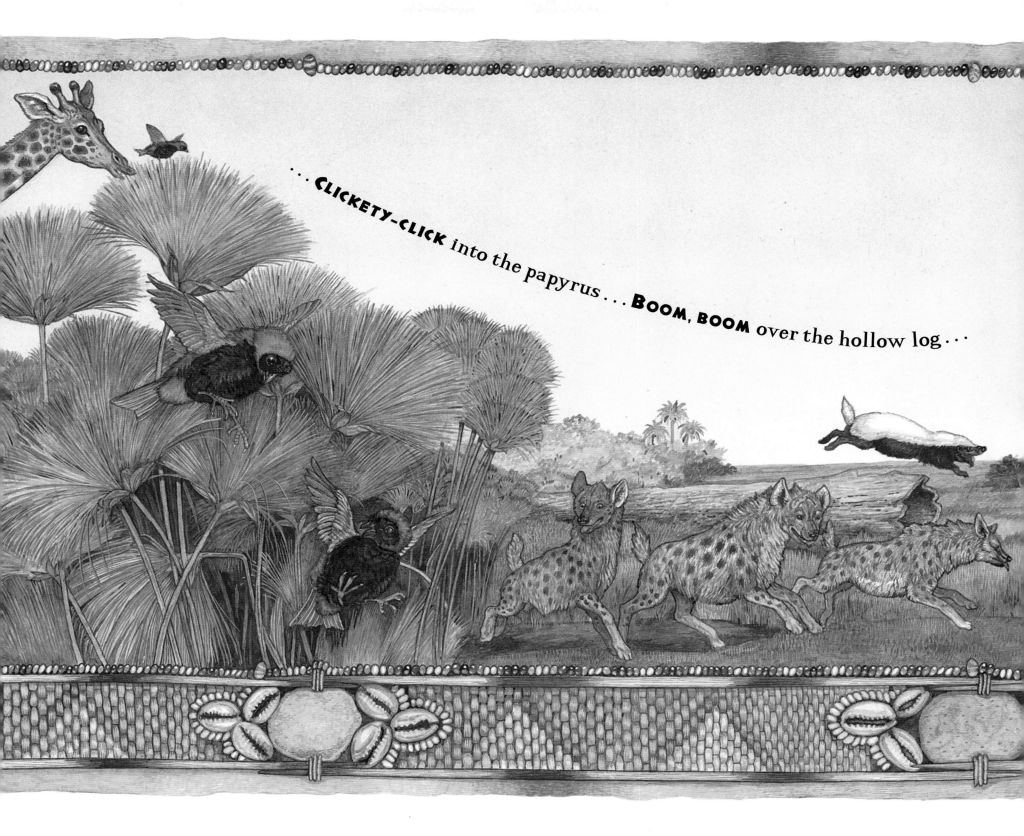

. . . **CLICKETY-CLICK** into the papyrus . . . **BOOM, BOOM** over the hollow log . . .

. . .**SPRONG** over the termite mound . . . **SPLISH**, **SPLASH** across the water hole . . .

. . . PITTER, PATTER over the baobab roots . . .

Badger dashed into his burrow. Honeyguide cheered.

In a flash Badger was as far from the entrance as he could be.

Right behind him was Lion's huge paw, batting the air.

But he could not reach him.

And that's the closest any animal could be to an angry lion and live to tell the tale.

That evening Mongoose squeaked to Elephant, who trumpeted
to Hippo, who bellowed to Warthog, who squealed to Bishop Bird,
who piped to Hyena, who whooped to Zebra, who snorted to Giraffe,
who was overheard by Guinea Hen, who bugled it far and wide.
It was the bush telegraph, and it said, "If Honeyguide leads you
to a beehive, be sure and reward her, or next time,
she will lead you to a lion!"

Other Puffin picture books by Jan Brett